The Eagle who was Afraid to Fly

Julene Bailie

DEDICATION

To Collin, my growing eagle. And to Pierce,
the newest member in our nest.

PROLOGUE

In the last Riverbend Eagle Tree book, "A Bully in the Nest", the sister eagle, "Sissy", fell from the eagle nest before she was ready to fly. Brother eagle helped his big sister climb up the tree to get back into the nest. "The Eagle who was Afraid to Fly", is the continuation of the dramatic story from the 2015 Riverbend Eagle nesting season.

JULENE BAILIE

Photo by Debbie Stika

Sister eagle, "Sissy", fell out of the Riverbend eagle nest before she learned how to fly. She sat alone on the lower branch of the tree for four days in the hot, July weather. Sissy had no food or water during this time. It was a very traumatic experience for her.

Brother eagle helped Sissy make it back up to the nest. Although Sissy was not hurt during the fall, something changed in her behavior. The big, brave, sister eagle that used to bully her little brother would not leave the nest. Even though Sissy was now old enough to fly, she was now afraid to try.

At first, papa and mama eagle did not know what was wrong with Sissy. They checked her over when she made it back to the nest. Although she was very hungry and thirsty, her wings and feathers seemed just fine. But then Sissy told papa eagle that she was afraid to fly.

Photo by Steven Arvid Gerde

The first two days after Sissy made it back to the nest, she just laid in the nest and cried for food. Papa eagle would go and bring food back to the nest for her. After all, Sissy was still his baby eagle no matter how old she was. Papa felt bad that Sissy had such a bad experience when she fell from the nest.

Photo by Ken Morain

In the meantime, brother eagle was actually flying. He would take off in the morning and would fly around with mama and papa during the day.

Sissy would watch her brother fly. He made it look so easy! But Sissy would not even consider flying. She was too afraid, and was staying in the big, cozy nest where she felt safe.

Over the next few days, the eagle family would leave the nest and would not come back for hours. Papa and mama eagle tried to encourage Sissy to go with them, but she refused.

Sissy just stayed in the nest alone, afraid to fly.

Photo by Debbie Stika

Each day, brother eagle flew from the nest with mama and papa eagle. He was learning all kinds of new things. Brother eagle returned to the nest with stories about his adventures. He was so excited to tell Sissy all the things he was doing outside of the nest, like flying over to the lakes to hunt and fish. He even got to take a bath, which was something Sissy had never experienced. Brother eagle really liked taking baths and playing in the water, especially since it was so hot out. He thought Sissy would be excited to try all these new things too, but she was not. Brother eagle just wished Sissy would go with him on these adventures.

Sissy was depressed and felt hopeless. Here she was, this big beautiful eagle and she was afraid to fly! Who ever heard of an eagle that was afraid to fly? Sissy laid in the nest and thought to herself, "Why am I so afraid to fly?" Sissy was no longer the strong, confident eagle she was before she fell from the nest. Now she was depressed, afraid, and doubted herself.

It was mama and papa eagle's job to get Sissy out of the nest and to teach her how to survive on her own. That is what parent eagles do. But no matter what they tried, they could not get Sissy motivated to leave the nest. They too began to feel helpless, and doubted themselves as eagle parents.

Brother eagle was doing great, and mama and papa eagle were happy with his progress. Now they had to figure out what to do to get Sissy out of the nest. Mama and papa would discuss Sissy's fear of flying. When Sissy overheard them talking about her issue, it made her feel bad that she was being such a problem.

After a week of Sissy laying around in the nest, papa eagle decided he needed to do something to help his little girl. Papa was perched on his resting branch close to the nest. In a gentle voice, he told Sissy that she needed to get over her fear. She was an eagle and was old enough to be out of the nest. Papa also told Sissy that all eagles had to learn to fly or they did not survive. He did not want her to panic, but she needed to know how serious the situation was. Papa figured that by telling Sissy these things, she might be motivated to leave the nest.

Sissy felt that papa did not understand how afraid she was. She wanted papa to keep taking care of her in the nest. Papa eagle's words about not surviving scared her even more. Sissy asked papa if she was going to survive. Papa said, "Sissy, I know you can fly. The thing is that YOU have to believe you can fly. I will do whatever I can to help you, but I cannot do it for you."

Sissy thought about what papa said, and knew it was true. The next day when brother eagle came back to the nest for the evening, she asked if he would help her to believe she could fly.

Brother eagle was confused. Sissy explained that if she did not believe she could fly, she would not be able to fly, and if she was not able to fly she would not survive. Brother eagle wanted his Sissy to survive so he agreed to help her. But he did not exactly know how to help.

Brother eagle had to come up with a plan. He decided the best thing to do was to wait until the next day to talk with mama and papa eagle. He figured they would have some ideas on how he could help Sissy.

Photo by Steven Arvid Gerde

The next day, mama, papa, and brother eagle flew down to the Green River. The temperature in the summer air was very hot, and the eagles frequently went to the river to take baths and cool off. Brother eagle told his parents he really wanted to help Sissy overcome her fear of flying. He said he needed their help to figure out what he should do to help Sissy believe in herself.

Mama said that believing in yourself came from building confidence. To build confidence, one of the things you had to do was practice. Papa agreed with mama eagle because she was usually right. Brother eagle just had to figure out how he could help build Sissy's confidence. He flew over to one of his favorite logs on the river so he could think.

Later that day, when brother eagle returned to the nest tree, he explained to Sissy that if he could fly she should be able to fly also. After all, they learned and practiced the same things while they were growing up. Sissy heard what brother eagle said, but she still did not think she could do it. Sissy was still afraid.

Brother eagle's talks with Sissy did not work. Just *telling* Sissy she could fly did not build her confidence. Brother eagle had to try something different. He came up with another idea to help Sissy. Brother eagle decided to explain *how* he flew. Brother eagle told Sissy that to fly, all she had to do was get up on the branch, flap her wings, and they would lift her into the sky. "That is how I do it," brother eagle said. Sissy was still not convinced she could fly. She could not imagine herself doing what brother eagle did.

That day, as brother eagle sat in the nest with Sissy, he kept thinking about what else he could do to help his big sister.

The next day, brother came up with yet another idea. "Sissy, you need to *watch* what I do when I take off to fly. Sure, it seems scary at first but it is easy once you know how to do it." Sissy spent that day watching her brother eagle launch himself from the big branch that extended out from the nest. This branch was big and strong, and was perfect for the eaglets to walk on. Brother eagle and Sissy nicknamed this big branch the "launching branch". Brother would climb up on the launching branch, stretch his big wings out, and lean forward. Then he would push off with his feet and would flap his wings and start to fly. Then he would come back and land in the tree. Brother eagle did this over and over so Sissy could watch how he launched and flew. But Sissy was still not convinced that she could fly. She was even afraid to get up onto the launching branch.

Brother eagle was getting very frustrated that Sissy would not try to fly. After all, he was flying and it was no big deal. He was spending lots of time showing her over, and over again, how he flew. Brother eagle got so frustrated he told Sissy that she was being a big baby eagle and should just stay in the nest. Then he flew off to go find some food with mama and papa.

Brother eagle's words hurt Sissy's feelings. She did not understand why her brother was upset with her, or why he said such hurtful things. Sissy sat in the nest the rest of the day all alone. Her family was out flying around and she wanted to be with them, but inside she was still too afraid to fly.

That day, the eagle family was gone for a very long time. Sissy had lots of time to think about flying. She cried herself to sleep because she was so sad about everything. Brother eagle was mad at her, mama and papa eagle were disappointed in her, and she was disappointed with herself. But then something happened. When Sissy fell asleep, she started dreaming about going up on the launching branch and flapping her wings like brother eagle showed her. Sissy could see herself up on the branch flapping her wings. It did not seem so scary in her dream. Sissy imagined what it would be like to be up on the branch. *Imagining* was an important step for Sissy in overcoming her fear, but she didn't know that yet.

When Sissy woke up, she decided to try walking up the launching branch. Sissy made up her mind she wanted to be with her family, and was determined to conquer her fear. Sissy did not realize that *making up her mind to take action* and being *determined* were also important steps in overcoming her fear.

Sissy carefully made her way up onto the launching branch. Her big, strong talons gripped the wood of the branch. Sissy held onto the branch real tight. She did not want to fall again.

When Sissy got to the end of the branch, she felt good about what she had just accomplished. Sissy practiced walking up and down the launching branch for hours, while her family was gone for the day. She did not realize that *practicing* was another important step in overcoming her fear. Practicing was helping Sissy build her confidence.

When the Riverbend eagle family came back to the nest that evening, Sissy was in the nest resting. She was exhausted from practicing on the launching branch all day, and was really happy papa brought some good food to the nest. Sissy was not ready to tell her brother that she had gone up on the launching branch. Brother eagle had not been very nice to her, so she went to bed early.

Brother eagle sat on the launching branch alone. He was still frustrated, but felt bad that he called Sissy a "big baby eagle".

The next day, instead of being sad and feeling sorry for herself, Sissy woke up and felt excited. She could not wait to practice on the branch some more! Sissy waited until her eagle family was out of sight and then she walked right up onto the launching branch. After all the practicing she did the day before, the launching branch did not seem scary at all. Sissy walked all the way to the end of the branch with confidence, and started thinking about what she should do next.

Sissy made up her mind she was going to practice flapping her wings - her eagle jumping jacks. Sissy remembered that brother eagle did this when he was getting ready to fly. At first, Sissy stayed in the nest and did not flap very hard. She stayed away from the edge of the nest so she wouldn't fall again. Sissy found the more she practiced, the easier it became. Sissy did not realize that she was learning another important lesson in overcoming her fear. She was breaking down the big task of flying into smaller steps. *Doing things in small steps* made a larger task easier to learn.

Sissy hopped up onto the launching branch and practiced doing eagle jumping jacks.

By the end of the day, Sissy was even climbing and hopping up on the branch that was higher than the launching branch! She was becoming a pro at jumping and walking on the branches.

When the eagle family returned to the nest at dinner time, brother eagle told Sissy he was sorry for calling her a big baby eagle. Sissy told brother eagle that his words really hurt her feelings. Brother eagle said he was sorry again. He told Sissy he was not only frustrated that she would not fly, but that he was also mad at himself because he could not help her fly. He felt he was a failure. Brother eagle said that he should not have taken his frustration out on her. Sissy agreed and forgave her brother eagle.

Sissy decided to tell brother eagle she had been practicing her wings and going up on the launching branch. Sissy said that watching him did help her, but she had to make up her mind to do it herself like papa said. Brother eagle was so surprised! He told Sissy how proud he was of her. That made Sissy feel really good. She asked brother eagle if he would share his launching techniques with her again the next day. Brother eagle agreed. He was ready to help Sissy again. Brother eagle telling Sissy he was proud of her accomplishments reinforced her desire to keep trying. Sissy didn't know it, but brother eagle's *praise for her accomplishments* was another important factor in helping her overcome her fear.

That evening, when they finished eating, the eaglets hung out in the nest together and thought about what they would do the next day.

The next day, brother eagle told mama and papa eagle he wanted to stay with Sissy in the nest. Mama and papa thought this was a bit strange, and wondered why. However, they decided the eaglets were old enough now to stay in the nest on their own. Mama and papa eagle took off to soar in the warm winds and beautiful blue sky.

As soon as mama and papa eagle left the nest, and were out of sight, Sissy said, "Come on, brother! Let me show you what I have been practicing!" And she hopped up on the launching branch and began flapping her big, beautiful wings.

Brother eagle was impressed. "Sissy, that is perfect! You are doing everything just right!" Sissy hopped back down into the nest and felt very good about herself. She was gaining more confidence.

"Brother, will you show me how you launch from the branch and how you land back in the tree again? I think if I watch you a few more times, I might be ready to try to fly." Brother eagle was very happy. He jumped up onto the launching branch. Sissy watched every move her brother made.

Brother eagle said, "Okay. Sissy – first you have to start flapping your wings like you did when you were practicing." But then he paused. "Oh wait! I forgot to tell you an important thing that papa taught me. You should always poop before you fly!" Sissy started laughing. Brother eagle said, "Seriously Sissy, papa said you should poop because it makes you lighter when you fly!" That made sense to Sissy. Brother eagle pooped.

Photo by Ken Morain

Brother eagle continued his lesson. "Now to launch, you need to lean forward, push off the branch with your feet, and keep flapping your wings. You will feel the air under your wings like you did when you were little. Your wings will lift you up into the air, like this!" Brother eagle leaned forward and pushed off the launching branch with his strong eagle feet. He kept flapping his wings and they lifted him up into the air.

Brother eagle flew around and landed back in the tree. Sissy said, "I think I got the part where you let go and flap your wings, but I am not too sure about the landing. Would you do it again, please?" And brother eagle showed Sissy how to put her legs and feet down and to reach in front of her so she could grab a branch to land on.

Brother eagle was happy to show Sissy as many times as it took to get her to be confident enough to fly. He launched, flew, and landed three more times. Each time, Sissy watched every move brother eagle made when he flew and landed. *Watching* brother eagle fly was helping Sissy learn what she needed to do to fly. Sissy closed her eyes and imagined she was making those same moves. She imagined herself lifting off the branch, flapping her big wings, and feeling the wind carry her. Sissy imagined putting her strong talons out in front of her to grab a branch so she could land, just like brother eagle showed her. *Imagining* doing the moves in her mind was another way Sissy was learning to overcome her fear.

When brother eagle came back to the tree the third time, Sissy said, "My turn! My turn! I want to try to fly! Brother, will you stay here with me?"

Brother eagle told Sissy he would stay right there. He really wanted to see his Sissy fly, and was hoping they could fly together. Brother eagle was as excited as Sissy was. He told Sissy, "Don't worry Sissy, I will be right here to catch you if you start to fall".

Sissy jumped up onto the launching branch with confidence. Brother eagle noticed a look of determination on Sissy's face that he had never seen before. This made him think of his big, strong sister the way she was before she fell out of the nest.

Sissy began to flap her wings, and flapped even harder. Then Sissy said, "Here I go!" She leaned out, pushed off the branch with her big, strong feet, flapped her wings, and Sissy flew.

Sissy's big wings carried her in the air over the fence to the golf course. She landed in a big evergreen tree. Her first landing was a bit awkward but she did it. People in the golf course, and the eagle watchers, watched as Sissy finally took her first flight.

Sissy hollered over to her brother, "I did it! I did it! I flew without falling! Wow! That was fun!" Brother eagle hollered back, "I knew you could do it, Sissy!"

Brother eagle flew over to an evergreen tree next to the tree that Sissy was in. His heart was filled with pride. He helped his sister learn how to fly and it made him feel really good. Brother eagle didn't know it, but teaching his sister how to fly helped to build his confidence too.

Brother eagle hollered out to Sissy, "Let's fly back to the nest and try again – but only if you want to." Sissy replied, "Oh, yes! I want to fly some more! Come on brother, let's go!" And she launched from the evergreen tree she was sitting in, flew over the fence, and back up to the nest tree. Sissy felt the wind under her wings again, and she liked it!

Sissy and brother eagle flew back and forth from the nest tree to different trees in the area. Sissy practiced her launches…

…and she practiced her landings.

And Sissy practiced some more. The more she practiced, the easier it was for Sissy to fly.

Photo by Ken Morain

The more they flew, the more confident Sissy felt. Once again, practicing helped Sissy to overcome her fear. By the end of the day, brother eagle and Sissy were not only flying together but they were playing in the air. They were having so much fun!

When mama and papa eagle returned to the nest that evening, Sissy could not wait to tell them her news. She jumped up and said, "Guess what, mama and papa? I am not afraid to fly anymore!"

Before mama or papa eagle could say anything, Sissy jumped up on the launching branch and flew around the tree. Mama and papa eagle could not believe it! Sissy was flying! They were both very proud of her.

And the fellow eagle watchers that were out watching the eagles that day saw her fly and were happy for her too.

Photo by Steven Arvid Gerde

For the rest of the season, the Riverbend Eagles enjoyed flying, hunting, and playing together.

Sissy was no longer the eagle who was afraid to fly. With the help of her family, and especially with the help of her brother eagle, she overcame her fear. Sissy transformed into a big, beautiful, confident eagle who could fly at last!

- The End -

EPILOGUE

The 2015 Riverbend Eagle season ended with both eaglets fledging and surviving the drama of growing up in the Riverbend Eagle Tree.

Mama and Papa Riverbend Eagle continued to expand their eagle family with two more eaglets in 2016. What adventures do the 2016 eaglets experience? Find out in the next book, "Garbage in the Nest", coming early 2018.

Until then, you can follow the journey of our Riverbend Eagles on the following online resources, or can visit us in person at the Riverbend Eagle Tree.

- Join our *Fellow Eagle Watchers* Facebook Group.
- Follow the *Riverbend Eagles* Facebook Page.
- See group photos of just the Riverbend Eagles on the *Riverbend Eagles* Flickr site.
- Watch narrated videos of the Riverbend Eagles (and other birds of prey) on Ralph Meier's *Sheeprugly* channel on You Tube.
- See photos from the individual photographers on their Facebook and Flickr sites

BALD EAGLE FREQUENTLY ASKED QUESTIONS (FAQS)

Below are some questions that the Fellow Eagle Watchers are asked from people that pass by the Riverbend Eagle Tree. We continue to learn more about these beautiful eagles each year as we observe them in the wild, and hope you enjoy learning about them too.

Q: How many eggs do a pair of Bald Eagles have each year?
A: The average for the west coast eagle populations is almost exactly two eggs per clutch. Eagles can lay only one egg but can also lay three eggs and there are some rare records of 4 eggs being laid. Most eagles only lay a single clutch of eggs. (Hancock Wildlife Org)

Q: After fledging, how do eaglets learn how to hunt?
A: After fledging, young eagles stay near the nest for six to nine weeks practicing their ability to fly and hunt. The eaglets have to learn by watching the parents and practicing.
(http://www.baldeagleinfo.com/eagle/eagle4.html)

Q: How do adult eagles feed their young?
A: The adult eagle shreds small pieces of meat from the prey with their beaks. The adult gently coaxes the tiny chick to take a morsel of meat from their beak. They will offer food again and again, eating rejected morsels themselves, and then tearing off another piece for the eaglet.
(http://www.baldeagleinfo.com/eagle/eagle4.html)

Q: How much weight can a bald eagle carry?
A: An adult eagle can lift only about 1/3 of its weight. Adults weigh between 10-14 pounds (females are heavier).
(https://www.nationaleaglecenter.org/eagle-nesting-young/)
(https://www.fws.gov/midwest/eagle/recovery/biologue.html)

Q: How many eagles are there in the United States?

A: According to the Department of Fish and Wildlife, there were 9,789 breeding pairs of bald eagles in the contingent U.S. in 2006, with 848 pairs in the state of Washington.
https://www.fws.gov/midwest/eagle/population/index.html

Q: How large is the territory for a nesting pair of bald eagles?

A: Eagle territory size varies by the availability of food. An average territory is about 1 mile in diameter.
http://www.learner.org/jnorth/tm/eagle/annual/facts_territory.html

Q: Do male and female eagles have different calls?

A: Females often times have a lower pitched call while the male tends to call with a higher pitch.
https://www.potawatomi.org/news/top-stories/1187-male-and-female-american-bald-eagles-similar-but-not-the-same

Q: How do eaglets get out of their eggs?

A: When the developing embryo is almost fully formed, it has developed a strong muscle on the back of its neck called a "hatching muscle", and a small sharp "egg tooth" on its upper beak. Hatching is a very physical process and a challenge that can take 2 to 4 days. It begins stretching and punctures the inner membrane with its beak at the blunt end of the egg, and for the first time breathes "air". The chick then slowly rotates counterclockwise by pivoting its legs and with the "egg tooth" scratches the inside of the shell. With the "hatching muscle" it punches a hole (called pipping) in the eggshell. With body movements and stretching the eaglet breaks the eggshell into two pieces and the hatching process is finally complete.
http://eaglenest.blogs.wm.edu/2010/03/05/how-do-i-get-out-of-this-egg/

Q: Do the Riverbend Eagles migrate?

A: Some biologists do not consider or characterize bald eagles as true "migrants", preferring to describe their movements away from and back toward their breeding territories as "seasonal movements". This is because almost all bald eagles only move away from their nesting areas as far as they need to to survive, meaning in order to find the food they need to survive. A great

many bald eagles, including the Riverbend eagles, never leave their general breeding areas because they don't need to, and remain there year-round.
https://www.learner.org/jnorth/tm/eagle/WeatherNye.html

Q: Why isn't there an eagle cam in the Riverbend eagle nest?
A: We would love to have a webcam in the Riverbend eagle tree! We have contacted some agencies to ask about this and don't quite have all the conditions met - yet. Maybe at some point we can continue to pursue this. To have a quality camera experience in a Bald Eagle nest requires quite a few conditions – at a minimum: weather-proof electrical power nearby the nest tree (or solar power suitability near the nest tree and cabling); secure internet access at the site (cable is preferred as most other systems do not provide a good viewing experience and are less reliable); and a safe tree/structure to climb and on which to mount the camera. Cameras must be installed outside of the nesting and territorial season, so between October and January in our area. And, for eagle nest cameras, coordination and permits depend on who operates the camera system.

OVERCOMING FEAR – DISCUSSION QUESTIONS

1. *In the story, mama eagle suggested that for brother eagle to help Sissy, he needed to help her build confidence so that she would overcome her fear. What did brother eagle do to help Sissy build her confidence?*

2. *Do you have other ideas that might have helped Sissy overcome her fear?*

3. *Have you ever been afraid to do something new, like learn to ride a bike, go to school, or speak in front of others?*

4. *In the story, Sissy dreamed about being on the launching branch, then, she imagined herself flying. Have you ever dreamed or imagined yourself doing something you were afraid of, before you actually did it?*

5. *Have you practiced or tried something you were afraid to do, then found it was not as bad as you thought it would be once you did it?*

6. *Have you ever overcome one of your fears? How did you do it? How did you feel once you conquered your fear?*

7. *Have you ever helped someone else overcome one of their fears? How did you feel when you helped them?*

MORE ABOUT FEAR

Fear is a natural emotion that everyone experiences. However, there are two types of fear – rational and irrational. *Rational* fears are those that help protect us from danger. For example, if you are standing too close to an edge on a cliff, you will probably experience fear. This fear is instinctual and is there to help you avoid danger, in this case, falling off the cliff. This is a helpful type of fear. *Irrational* fears are those that we experience when we are not really in danger. For example, being afraid of speaking in front of others. It is the irrational fears that keep us from living our life and that we need to learn to overcome.

If you are not sure if the fear you are experiencing is rational or irrational, or if you would like to find out how to overcome an irrational fear, there are many resources available to you. Talk to an adult about your fear, and ask them to help you find the resource that is right for you.

There are many books on this subject, as well as websites that are devoted to this topic. Don't let your fears hold you back. Getting over a fear is a skill that anyone can learn.

ACKNOWLEDGMENTS

A special thank you to the following individuals for their contribution to this book. Collin Anderson, my eagle-eye editor; photographers and awesome friends Ken Morain, Debbie Burrous Stika, and Steven Arvid Gerde, who supplied pictures needed to complete this story where my collection was lacking; my family who never seem to tire of my endless eagle stories; and to all the Fellow Eagle Watchers who are a blast to hang out with. I would be remiss in not mentioning my two cats, Keesa and Khaleesi, who keep me company as I write and wonder why I sometimes pay more attention to my keyboard than to them.

More special thanks to you, my readers, who inspire me to continue telling stories about the Riverbend Eagles. It is fun sharing information about this special family of eagles. I hope you enjoy reading about them as much as I do writing about them.

And to the Riverbend Eagles – my inspiration. May you fly high and free for many years to come.

Made in the USA
San Bernardino, CA
17 January 2018